WITCHES, WIZARDS AND MAGICAL PEOPLE

BY JOHN PATIENCE

PUBLISHED BY PETER HADDOCK LIMITED,
BRIDLINGTON, ENGLAND.

PRINTED IN U.A.E.

Hubble

A BOOK OF WITCHES & WIZARDS

Bubble

BY JOHN PATIENCE

The Witch Next Door

Amy's father had been given a new job in a new town and the family had just moved house. It was all rather frightening for Amy. She had left all her old friends behind and the children who were playing in the street didn't seem to want to know her. She went out and stood at the garden gate, watching them and hoping that they would invite her over to play, but they didn't. One of them even began to make faces at her and call her names. When she went down to the shop for her mother, two big boys jumped out at her from an alleyway, making her drop the shopping. Then they chased her all the way home.

Amy's mother did her best to make her feel better, but that night Amy lay in bed wishing she was back in her old house surrounded by her old friends. Then something happened to make her forget her troubles. She heard a funny sort of noise outside her window. Tiptoeing across her room, she peeped out through the curtains and saw the strangest thing. The woman who lived next door was flying around the sky on her vacuum cleaner! The first time she had seen that woman Amy had guessed that there was something funny about her – she had spiky red hair, wore weird make-up and peculiar clothes. "Of course," whispered Amy, "she's a witch!"

The next morning at breakfast Amy told her mother and father about the witch next door, but they just laughed and told her not to be so silly. "There's no such thing as witches," said her mother. "Look, there's a letter for the lady next door. The postman delivered it to our house by mistake. Take it round for me, there's a good girl." Well, Amy was not too happy about that, but she did as she was told. She took the letter, which was addressed to Mrs. Moon, and knocked on her door. The loud music which had been playing in the house was turned off and, through the coloured glass in the front door Amy could see the witch coming down the hallway. Then the door opened. "Hello. You're the little girl next door, aren't you?" said the witch. "Is that letter for me? That postman! He's a real daydreamer. Come in – we'll get to know each other." Amy was completely tongue-tied, but she followed the witch into the house. And a very funny house it was, too, with all sorts of strange posters and paintings on the walls, and all kinds of junk lying around everywhere. "Don't mind the mess," said the witch cheerily. "I'll get around to tidying it up some day." And she led Amy into the kitchen and there was the witch's black cat, curled up on a chair. But the room was warm and friendly, and Amy's fears began to melt away. Maybe Mrs. Moon was a good witch, a white witch. There was a wonderful smell in the kitchen of newly baked bread. Mrs. Moon cut a big slice off the loaf, spread lots of butter and jam on it and gave it to Amy. "Try that," she said. "I think it's the best I've ever baked." Amy took a bite and at that moment, as if by magic, she and the witch became the best of friends and Amy was telling Mrs. Moon all kinds of things about where she came from and how she couldn't make friends with the other children in the street.

"Don't worry," said Mrs. Moon. "You'll have no more trouble. I've got something special for you. Here it is. It's a magic woolly hat – I knitted it myself. When you put

this hat on your head you will turn into a little monster and you'll never be afraid of anyone again. After all, no-one chases monsters, do they? But be a good monster – don't go round frightening everybody, will you?" "No, I wouldn't do that," promised Amy. Then she put on the woolly hat, turned into a monster and went home.

"Hello, Mum. I'm a monster," said Amy. "So you are,"

said Amy's mother. "Would you go down to the shop for some washing powder dear?" "Sure," said Amy. She knew that no-one would chase her now, so she was feeling pleased with herself and full of confidence. In the street she smiled a great big monster smile and the other children smiled back at her. "Hi!" they said. "Do you want to play with us?" "Later," said Amy. "I'm a monster and I'm going down to the shop for my Mum." Being a monster was really great – the best thing ever! Amy leapt up into the air, swung around a road sign and ran off down the pavement.

As Amy was on her way back from the shop, the two big boys tried to scare her again, but she gave a terrible, fierce monster roar and they both ran away. After that she went to play with the other children. They thought that they would like to be monsters too, so they all pretended. Then there were lots of little monsters leaping around all over the place though, of course, Amy was the best because she was wearing her magic monster hat.

Now Amy was happy. She had made lots of new friends, but her very best friend of all was Mrs. Moon. That night she saw her whizzing around the sky on her vacuum cleaner again, sucking up the stars as if they were crumbs on the carpet. She tapped on the window and waved and Mrs. Moon waved back. Then Amy put on her monster hat, curled up in bed and fell asleep.

Esmeralda

smeralda was a witch's cat,
But found it none too easy.
Looping loops and swooping swoops —
It made her feel quite queasy.
And one wild night, by pale moonlight,
Green with travel sickness,
She lost her grip, began to slip
And found herself broomstickless.
Where she fell it's strange to tell.
It's weird to be relating.
Down my chimney pot the feline shot,
Her speed accelerating.
Now, it's no joke to be awoke
By wild things from the chimney.
My heart went BUMP, it made me jump,
It made me shout, "By Jimmeny!"
But you'd never guess her origins
From looking at her now.
She's just like any other cat,
The same purr and meow.
There's just that look she gives you,
The one that makes you quiver,
Shudder, shake, turn cold and quake,
Tremble, squirm and shiver!

Good Neighbours

At the end of Badger Lane there stood two adjoining cottages. A witch lived in one of them and her next-door-neighbour was a wizard. They had never been on good terms, in fact, to be quite blunt, they hated each other. The witch was forever brewing up really foul-smelling potions and those smells always found their way into the wizard's house.

One morning, when there was a very bad smell in the air, the wizard noticed that the witch was out in her garden, presumably collecting some more rubbish to add to her concoction. Stalking out into his own garden, the wizard leaned across the fence and said, "Oh, look! There's a lovely slimy snail, and there's a nice juicy worm, and goodness me, don't miss that fat little frog!" "Keep your remarks to yourself, you old fool," sneered the witch. "Keep your smells to yourself, then," shouted the wizard. "You horrible old bat!" "Old bat, am I? At least I don't keep people awake all night, chanting stupid spells and dancing around like a demented donkey. You're a useless wizard, anyway. You couldn't cast a proper spell to save your life!" This was too much for the wizard. "We'll see about that," he muttered darkly. "We'll see about that."

The wizard pored over his spell books all night long. It was ages since he had worked any really powerful magic.

Mostly, he earned his living by vanishing warts from the end of people's noses and that sort of thing. But now he was looking for something special, something extremely impressive and eventually he found it.

The next morning he confronted the witch over the garden fence again. "Couldn't cast a spell to save my life, eh?" he said. "Watch this, then." And he began to chant something like this:

> "Elgnuj, elgnuj, round about
> Mumbo jumbo, inside out,
> Tac to oppih, oppih pot,
> Turn around and watchagot?"

Then, in an instant, it happened. The witch's garden was transformed into a tropical jungle and her cat, which had been toying with a mouse, was changed into (of all things) a hippopotamus! The witch was beside herself with rage.

She waved her wand in the air and shrieked out some bizarre magic spell of her own. The wizard's beard turned green, his ears grew long and furry like a donkey's. Then he blew up like a balloon and floated up into the air.

Well, that was the beginning of the magic war. Soon the witch and the wizard were casting all kinds of spells on each other. First, the witch's broomstick caught fire.

The wizard's chair jumped up and ran away with him. Then a plague of nasty little nameless creatures came down the chimney, chased the witch all around her house and pinched her black and blue.

This sort of nonsense couldn't go on for ever, of course, and it happened that they both decided at the very same time to put an end to it with the very best spell they could conjure up. "I'll show the old crone," thought the wizard. "I'll teach the silly old fool," muttered the witch. And while the wizard scoured his magic books for a spell to end all spells, the witch threw everything she could find into her bubbling cauldron.

The wizard looked pale-faced and grim as he stood in his garden the following morning. He stretched out his arms towards the witch and began to chant the terrible spell he had learned:

"All things black and horrible,
Mischief from the night,
Slimy things, and grimy things
And rhymes that aren't quite right,
Toothache and the collywobbles,
Mumps and the chickenpox,
Boils and warts and thingummybobs
And nasty-smelling socks."

As he spoke, coloured smoke started to pour out from his fingertips, and the witch realised that she had better hurry up and work her own magic. She took a bottle filled with her magic potion from under her cape and, taking off the stopper, threw it at the wizard. "Magic, do your stuff!" she cried. And if a drop of the potion had touched the wizard it might well have turned him into a toad, but it didn't. The witch's and the wizard's magic met and mixed in mid air and something remarkable happened. There was a smash, a crash, a splash and a flash and a terrible monster appeared. It had four great bulging eyes, terrible claws and a mouth full of horrible, yellow teeth. And it roared like a lion. It smashed down the fence and chased the terrified witch and wizard all around their gardens. Around and around they ran with the dreadful monster rushing after them, until, at last, completely exhausted and imagining

that at any minute they would both be gobbled up, they fell down on their knees. "I'm sorry," panted the witch. "It's all my fault." "No, no. It's my fault," puffed the wizard. "I'm sorry."

"Sorry, sorry, sorry. Did you say sorry?" bellowed the monster, turning horribly pale. "Yes, that's right, sorry," cried the wizard, realising that he had discovered the magic word. "Sorry, sorry, sorry!" shouted the witch and the wizard together, dancing around and hugging each other. Then the monster began to shake and tremble quite uncontrollably. He shook so violently that he shook himself to pieces and crumbled into a pile of dust.

From that day on, the witch and the wizard became the very best of friends and often popped into each other's houses for a cup of tea and to exchange spells.

The Frog Prince

Oh, a happy little frog, was I,
Sitting in my ditch,
Croaking at the clear blue sky,
When along came a wicked witch.
She cast an evil spell on me,
To think of it makes me wince,
She turned me in an instant
Into a handsome prince.
Now I must leave my froggy friends
It's time to go, I guess.
I must bid farewell to contentment,
And marry some silly princess!

Simple Jack and the Wizard

There was once a poor boy named Jack who earned his living as a street musician. He wore tattered, ragged clothes, but a happy smile. The rich people of the town laughed at Jack. They jeered at him from their coaches as they rode by. They called him "simple." But Jack didn't mind. He made enough money to buy himself food and drink and keep a roof over his head.

One day a wizard came to the town where Jack lived and, standing in the square, he threw his arms into the air and brought down a tremendous bolt of lightning. "I am your ruler," he shouted. "From this moment you are all my slaves. You will work for me. I will see that you have all the food you need and I will give you clothes to wear, but if you do not obey me, I will kill you all!"

It seemed that there was very little choice. The wizard must be obeyed. He commanded the townsfolk to build him a great tower of glittering gold in the square and kept them working at it day and night. Then, when it was completed, he took up residence and from its high balcony he was able to keep watch on the entire town to see that no-one disobeyed his laws. These were some of the laws:

There will be no smiling or laughing.

Children will not play games in the streets, and

There will be absolutely NO music.

Well, the people obeyed all these terrible laws and the wizard gave them food to eat and clothes to wear, but the food which he conjured out of thin air tasted of nothing at

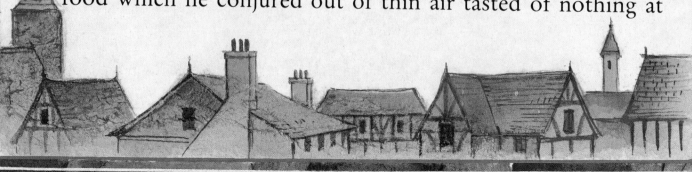

all and did not satisfy anyone's hunger, and the clothes he gave them were drab grey and didn't keep out the cold.

At last the townsfolk couldn't stand it any longer. They gathered at the golden tower to confront the wizard. "We are unhappy," they moaned. "Your laws are stupid and pointless." This made the wizard extremely angry and, with a sweep of his arm, he magically summoned up three great trolls, who threatened everyone, and patrolled the town to make sure that no-one else got any silly ideas about being happy.

But what had become of Simple Jack? Well now, I doubt if there was anyone in that whole, unhappy town more unhappy than poor Jack. Now that he was no longer allowed to play his pipe in the streets, his cheerful smile had disappeared like the sun behind a big, grey cloud. But Jack had courage and he decided that he must go to see the

wizard. "After all," thought Jack, 'I have nothing to lose. The wizard has made life so miserable that it is hardly worth living."

Jack knocked loudly on the door of the golden tower and soon the wizard appeared. "What do you want?" he growled. "Why aren't you working with the other townsfolk?" The wizard had commanded that everyone should begin working at a great carving of himself which was to be hewn out of the side of a mountain which overlooked the town. They had been slaving away at it for months, watched over by the three trolls. "I'm not interested in carving statues. I want to play my pipe in the streets the way I used to," replied Jack bravely. At this, the wizard roared with anger and, chanting a spell, magicked into being, a terrifying, fire-breathing thingummybob. Anyone else would have turned and run, but Jack stood his ground. He had begun to realise

something about the wizard. His magic was all illusion, it had no substance. The food he gave did not fill the people's stomachs or satisfy their hunger. The clothes did not keep them warm. And, come to think of it, that bolt of lightning he had brought down had hit a dog and it hadn't even scratched it.

Jack decided to put his idea to the test. Putting his pipe to his lips, he began to play and as the forbidden music filled the air, the monster began to shrink smaller and smaller and smaller until eventually it was no bigger than a mouse, at which point it took fright and ran away. (If anyone is interested, I think it was caught and eaten by a cat.) "Go away or I'll, I'll, I'll . . . I don't know what I'll do!" screamed the wizard. "You're just a fraud," said Jack and he started to laugh. The wizard was mortified, no-one had ever dared to laugh at him before. The sound stabbed him like a knife. He let out a horrible scream and, beginning at his toes and working upwards, he began to fade away, until . . . at last only his head remained, floating in the air. And then that, too, turned into a mist and was blown away. And the wizard was never seen or heard of again.

The trolls disappeared along with the wizard and everyone was free again. The children played games in the streets. People laughed and joked and – best of all as far as he was concerned – Jack was able to go back to playing his pipe. Actually, the townsfolk wanted to make him Lord Mayor and dress him up in fine clothes, but he refused. You might think that was stupid of him, but he was happy just the way he was. And as a matter of fact, people stopped calling him Simple Jack after that and named him Happy Jack instead.

Dragon Tales

A BOOK OF DRAGONS
BY JOHN PATIENCE

Mr Pringle and the Dragon

After retiring from his job at the paint factory, Mr Pringle became bored and decided to become an odd job man. He wrote out a card and put it in the window of the corner shop. The card read:

Odd Jobs
No job is too big. No job is too small.
Contact: Mr Pringle, 13 Station Road.

The next morning, as Mr Pringle was enjoying a nice cup of tea, his doorbell rang and there, on his doorstep stood his first client! "Good morning," she said politely. "I'm the Witch of Far Away and Long Ago. I saw your card in the shop window and I have a little job for you. It's not much really, just a bothersome dragon that needs slaying in Long Ago. I'd do it myself but I'm busy in Far Away." "Well, dragon-slaying is not exactly my line of work," said Mr Pringle cautiously. He suspected that this might be some kind of practical joke. "Anyway, shouldn't I have a magic sword to do the slaying with?" "Cats and broomsticks!" cried the Witch. "You're quite right – I've forgotten to bring the sword. Oh well, it can't be helped. You'll have to make do with this." The Witch plucked a long silver pin from her pointed hat and handed it to Mr Pringle. "Here, just a minute," he began. "Sorry, I must be flying," said the Witch. "And so must you. Good luck." And, saying this, she blew at Mr Pringle as you might blow at a dandelion clock.

It was only a little puff of breath, but it blew Mr Pringle right off his feet and clean out of this world. Head over heels he spun, through swirling clouds of rainbow mist. His head was filled with a sound like tinkling wind chimes and he tingled from head to foot. "Stop! Stop!" cried the old man, and quite suddenly everything went still. The mist cleared and he found himself standing in the middle of a beautiful, fairytale city.

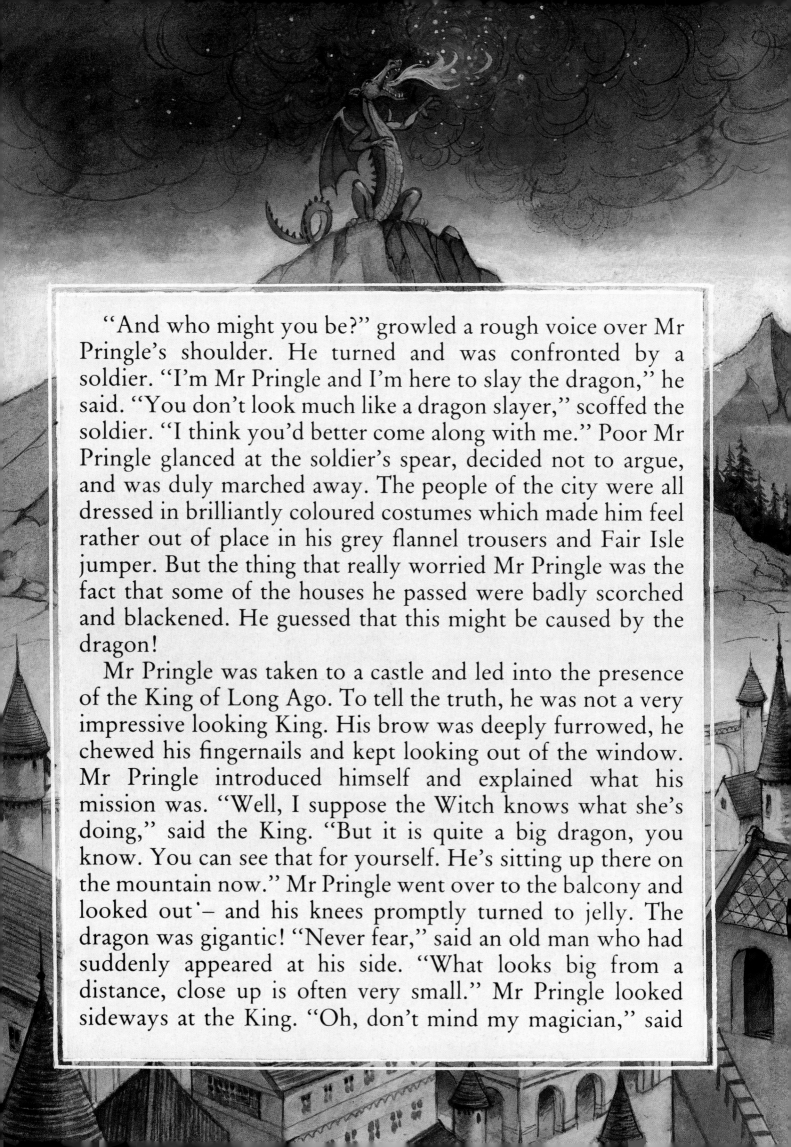

"And who might you be?" growled a rough voice over Mr Pringle's shoulder. He turned and was confronted by a soldier. "I'm Mr Pringle and I'm here to slay the dragon," he said. "You don't look much like a dragon slayer," scoffed the soldier. "I think you'd better come along with me." Poor Mr Pringle glanced at the soldier's spear, decided not to argue, and was duly marched away. The people of the city were all dressed in brilliantly coloured costumes which made him feel rather out of place in his grey flannel trousers and Fair Isle jumper. But the thing that really worried Mr Pringle was the fact that some of the houses he passed were badly scorched and blackened. He guessed that this might be caused by the dragon!

Mr Pringle was taken to a castle and led into the presence of the King of Long Ago. To tell the truth, he was not a very impressive looking King. His brow was deeply furrowed, he chewed his fingernails and kept looking out of the window. Mr Pringle introduced himself and explained what his mission was. "Well, I suppose the Witch knows what she's doing," said the King. "But it is quite a big dragon, you know. You can see that for yourself. He's sitting up there on the mountain now." Mr Pringle went over to the balcony and looked out – and his knees promptly turned to jelly. The dragon was gigantic! "Never fear," said an old man who had suddenly appeared at his side. "What looks big from a distance, close up is often very small." Mr Pringle looked sideways at the King. "Oh, don't mind my magician," said

the King. "He's always saying things like that. I think they're supposed to make him sound wise, the way proper magicians do in fairytales. He isn't magic at all really."

Some time later, up on the mountain top, the dragon narrowed his cruel, yellow eyes, and watched a tiny, balding figure walk out through the city gates, pick his way across the wasteland between the city and the mountain, and begin to climb. The figure was Mr Pringle.

Though he was very frightened he had decided that he could not allow himself to be defeated by the first odd job that came his way. It could be very bad for his reputation! Mr Pringle climbed and climbed and at last, there he stood, trembling before the enormous, monstrous, fearsome, terrible, beasticalburbulating, fire-breathing foe! "What do you want?" hissed the dragon. "Well, actually, I've come to slay you," replied Mr Pringle. "But I don't much like violence. I'll tell you what, why don't you just fly away like a good dragon and save all the nastiness?" The dragon laughed. A great horrible laugh it was, that sounded like the bubbling of a volcano. "No! I'll tell YOU what," he roared. "Just for fun, we'll play by fairytale rules; you ask me three riddles and if I can't guess them I'll fly away. If I do guess them, I'll eat you up. How's that?" "Alright," agreed Mr Pringle. "I've got one for you: What's white and swings through the jungle?" The dragon puffed a few smoke rings and thought for a while. "I don't know," he admitted, sulkily. "A meringue-utang," said Mr Pringle. "Here's the second one: What's black and white and red all over?" Again, the dragon paused for thought. "I don't know," he growled at last. "A newspaper," said Mr Pringle. "Now here's the last one: What's long, bent and yellow and travels at ninety miles an hour?" "I don't know," roared the dragon at the top of his terrible voice. "A jet-propelled banana!" cried Mr Pringle triumphantly. "I win. Now off you go, bye bye." "Rubbish!" snapped the dragon, snatching Mr Pringle up in one of his fearsome great claws. "Those weren't proper riddles – they were only jokes. I'm going to eat you up." Mr Pringle wished hard at that moment that he had a magic sword, but instead he found only the Witch's hat pin. Desperately, he plunged it into the end of the dragon's

nose. "Take that!" he cried. There was a loud bang, a shower of coloured sparks, and Mr Pringle was sent flying head over heels. He was spinning back through the swirling rainbow coloured mists with which he had become acquainted at the start of his adventure. But instead of the sound of the wind chimes in his ears, he heard a voice saying, over and over again, "Letter for you, Mr Pringle. Letter for you, Mr Pringle."

Shortly he came to his senses and discovered himself to be standing back on his own doorstep. In front of him was the postman. "Letter for you, Mr Pringle," he was saying. Mr Pringle took the letter absentmindedly. Had it all been a dream? Yes, it must have been. Shaking his head, he opened the letter and found a cheque inside it, for ONE THOUSAND GOLD COINS. The old man gasped. It was signed by the Witch of Long Ago and Far Away and on the back of it was scribbled, "For the slaying of one bothersome dragon."

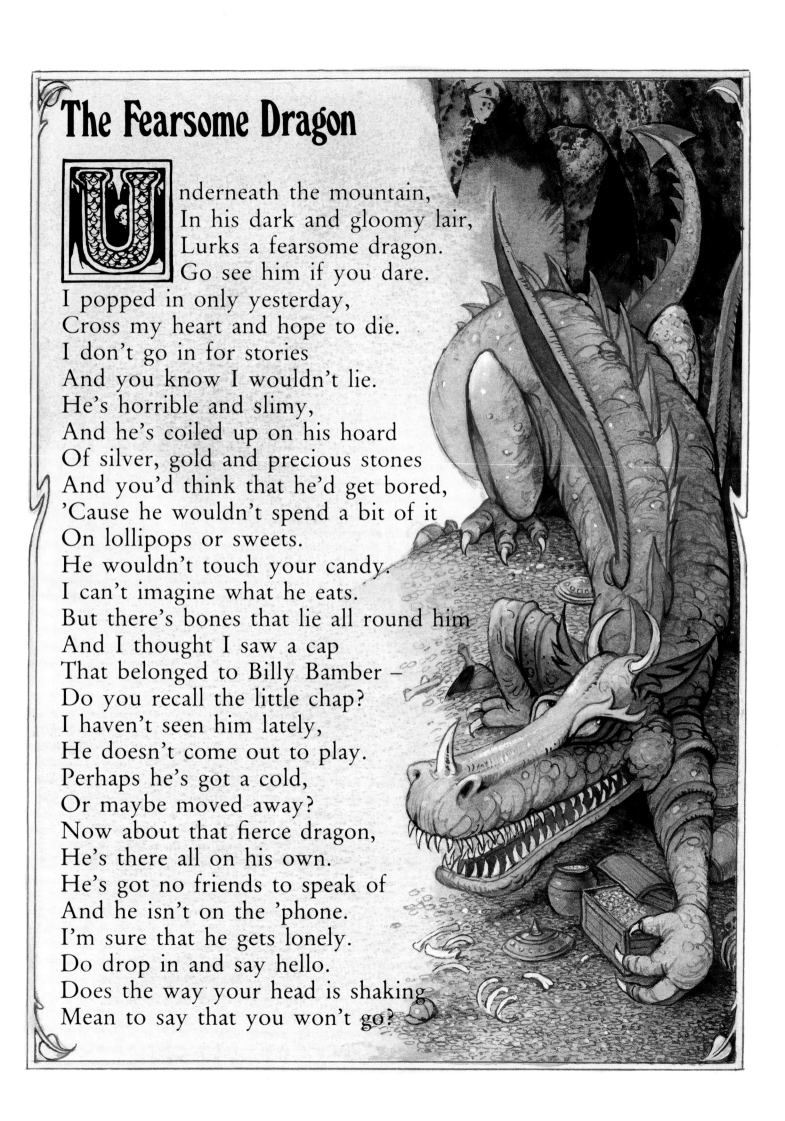

The Fearsome Dragon

Underneath the mountain,
In his dark and gloomy lair,
Lurks a fearsome dragon.
Go see him if you dare.
I popped in only yesterday,
Cross my heart and hope to die.
I don't go in for stories
And you know I wouldn't lie.
He's horrible and slimy,
And he's coiled up on his hoard
Of silver, gold and precious stones
And you'd think that he'd get bored,
'Cause he wouldn't spend a bit of it
On lollipops or sweets.
He wouldn't touch your candy.
I can't imagine what he eats.
But there's bones that lie all round him
And I thought I saw a cap
That belonged to Billy Bamber –
Do you recall the little chap?
I haven't seen him lately,
He doesn't come out to play.
Perhaps he's got a cold,
Or maybe moved away?
Now about that fierce dragon,
He's there all on his own.
He's got no friends to speak of
And he isn't on the 'phone.
I'm sure that he gets lonely.
Do drop in and say hello.
Does the way your head is shaking
Mean to say that you won't go?

The Enchanted Rock

There was once a dragon who flew down and settled upon an enchanted rock and was turned immediately to stone. The rain and the snow fell upon him, the wind lashed around him and the sun beat down upon his scaly head, but he never blinked an eyelid. One by one, the years passed and a great city grew up around the stone dragon. The people of the city supposed that he was nothing more than a statue, but he watched everything that happened. He saw how unhappy the people were becoming. He listened to them talking, complaining that they had no money because King Skinflint taxed them so harshly that their children were starving and went without shoes. And if anyone had looked closely at the dragon they would have seen tears welling up in his stone eyes and trickling down his cheeks, because inside his great stone body the dragon had a heart as soft as a marshmallow and he felt sorry for the poor people.

Then one morning, as the sun rose, a wisp of smoke curled up from the dragon's nostrils. Slowly, he moved his head from side to side, stretched out his wings and came alive again. A thousand years had passed and that's as long as even the strongest magic lasts. Now the dragon was free he decided that it was high time things were put right in the city, so he flew to King Skinflint's castle. The King was in his counting house, counting out his money when in flew the dragon. It gave him such a fright that he knocked over all his nice, neat piles of gold coins. "Help! I'm being attacked by a dragon," screamed the King. The door burst open and in

rushed a group of guards, armed with swords and spears. "There's no need for all this," said the dragon. "I'm sure we can both be reasonable." "What do you mean?" said King Skinflint gruffly. "Explain yourself quickly. Time is money. That's one gold coin you've cost me already!" "Well you know your subjects are all starving," explained the dragon. "I think you should stop taxing them. You have plenty of gold already – your counting house is full of it." "Don't be stupid!" shrieked the King, his eyes almost popping out of his head. "I need all the gold I can get. Anyway, money is too good for poor people." As he said this the King suddenly

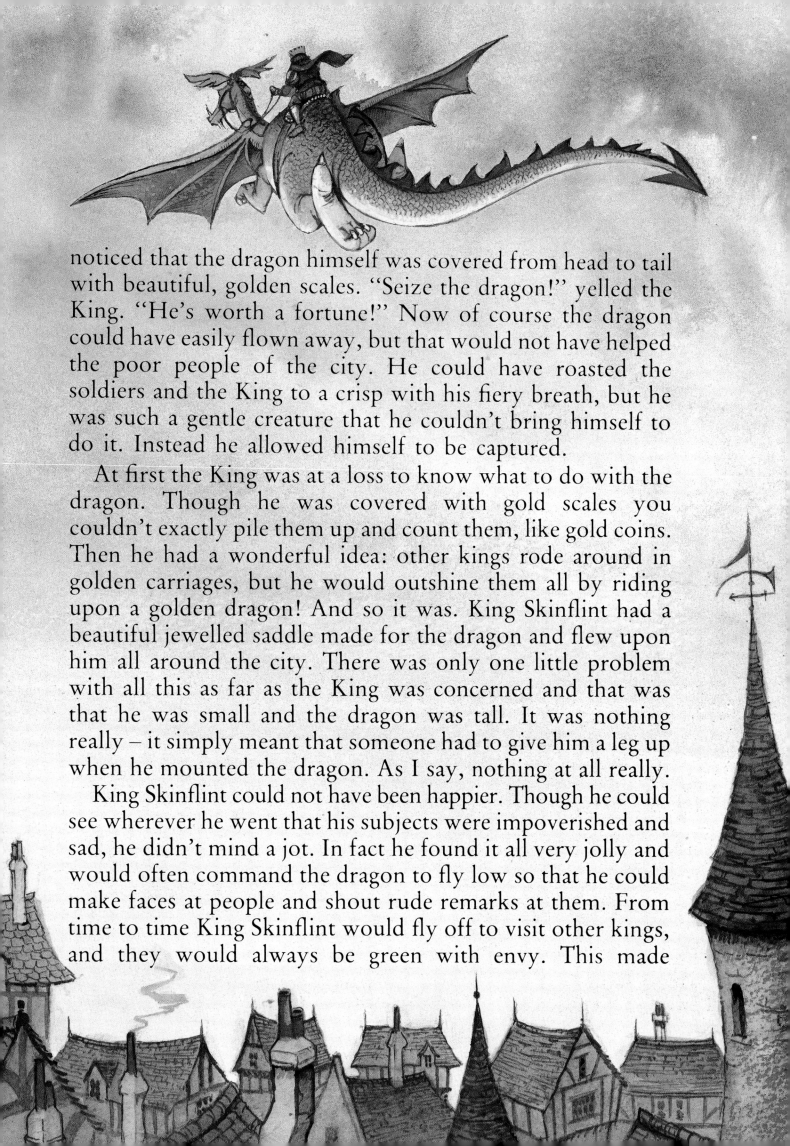

noticed that the dragon himself was covered from head to tail with beautiful, golden scales. "Seize the dragon!" yelled the King. "He's worth a fortune!" Now of course the dragon could have easily flown away, but that would not have helped the poor people of the city. He could have roasted the soldiers and the King to a crisp with his fiery breath, but he was such a gentle creature that he couldn't bring himself to do it. Instead he allowed himself to be captured.

At first the King was at a loss to know what to do with the dragon. Though he was covered with gold scales you couldn't exactly pile them up and count them, like gold coins. Then he had a wonderful idea: other kings rode around in golden carriages, but he would outshine them all by riding upon a golden dragon! And so it was. King Skinflint had a beautiful jewelled saddle made for the dragon and flew upon him all around the city. There was only one little problem with all this as far as the King was concerned and that was that he was small and the dragon was tall. It was nothing really – it simply meant that someone had to give him a leg up when he mounted the dragon. As I say, nothing at all really.

King Skinflint could not have been happier. Though he could see wherever he went that his subjects were impoverished and sad, he didn't mind a jot. In fact he found it all very jolly and would often command the dragon to fly low so that he could make faces at people and shout rude remarks at them. From time to time King Skinflint would fly off to visit other kings, and they would always be green with envy. This made

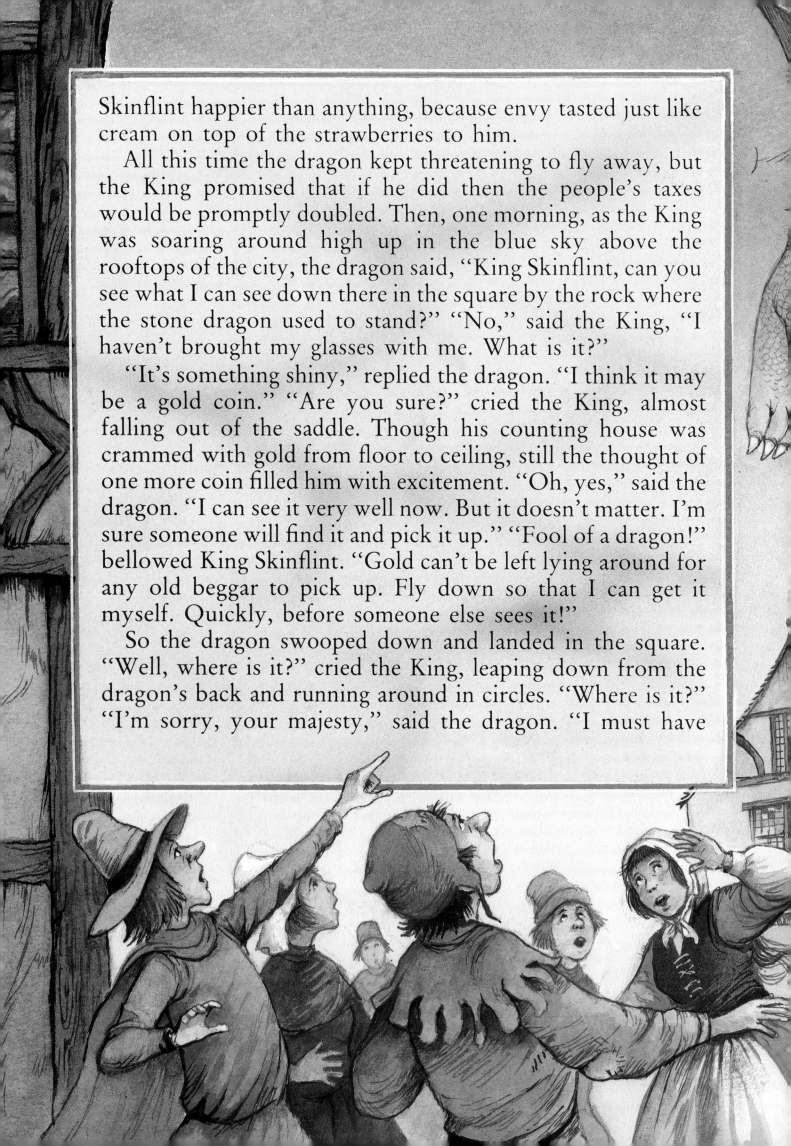

Skinflint happier than anything, because envy tasted just like cream on top of the strawberries to him.

All this time the dragon kept threatening to fly away, but the King promised that if he did then the people's taxes would be promptly doubled. Then, one morning, as the King was soaring around high up in the blue sky above the rooftops of the city, the dragon said, "King Skinflint, can you see what I can see down there in the square by the rock where the stone dragon used to stand?" "No," said the King, "I haven't brought my glasses with me. What is it?"

"It's something shiny," replied the dragon. "I think it may be a gold coin." "Are you sure?" cried the King, almost falling out of the saddle. Though his counting house was crammed with gold from floor to ceiling, still the thought of one more coin filled him with excitement. "Oh, yes," said the dragon. "I can see it very well now. But it doesn't matter. I'm sure someone will find it and pick it up." "Fool of a dragon!" bellowed King Skinflint. "Gold can't be left lying around for any old beggar to pick up. Fly down so that I can get it myself. Quickly, before someone else sees it!"

So the dragon swooped down and landed in the square. "Well, where is it?" cried the King, leaping down from the dragon's back and running around in circles. "Where is it?" "I'm sorry, your majesty," said the dragon. "I must have

been mistaken. Perhaps it was just a piece of broken glass catching the sunlight." "Idiot!" roared the King. "Take me back to the palace at once. I wish to count my money again to cheer myself up." "Very well, climb on my back," said the dragon. The King looked around for someone to give him a leg up, but no-one offered to help. Why should they? He had never helped them. "I'll teach you all," shouted King Skinflint. "I'll triple your taxes tomorrow!" "Perhaps you could climb up on that rock," suggested the dragon, "and hop on my back from there." "Very well," replied the King. He was not used to climbing but needs must, so, huffing and puffing, he struggled up the enchanted rock and, standing on top, he immediately turned to stone. He could not move a muscle, nor bat an eyelid, nor speak a word. "Don't worry," said the dragon. "The enchantment will wear off in a thousand years. That will give you lots of time to think about how greedy you have been."

Then the dragon beat his great wings and rose up into the air. In a little while he was back in the King's counting house. There he picked up a sack of gold and away he flew with it, down the city streets, showering down gold coins wherever he went. All day long he flew back and forth between the counting house and the city streets until at last all the King's gold had been given back to the people. From that day on, no-one was ever poor in the city again and, believe it or not, the dragon was made King!

My Pet

The annual competition
For the most interesting pet,
Was held upon the village green
And judged by the local Vet.
There were cats and dogs
And guinea pigs
And hamsters by the score.
There were parrots, rabbits and goldfish
(Which are really quite a bore).
Tadpoles in jars and spiders from Mars
(At least, Tom said they were),
A pony and a donkey,
A goat and something rare.
A pelican pinched the third prize,
And a python squeezed in second,
But my pet won the first prize,
'Cause everybody reckoned
He's the best pet that there ever was,
A thing that's seldom seen.
He's a great big scary dragon,
All scaly, weird and green!

Where have all the Dragons gone

There was once a dragon called Embers who lived in a cave by the deep, green sea. Every day a little boy would come to play with him and every night the sea would sing him a lullaby. And Embers was very happy.

Then one evening after the little boy, whose name was Joseph, had gone home, Embers lay down in his cave to sleep, and the sea began to sing its song. But this time the song was different:

"Hunt high and low and you won't find a one,
all of the dragons but Embers are gone.
Search far and wide, they're vanished away,
like mist in the morning, like a lost summer's day.
No fiery breath, no scaly green face,
the dragons have flown and left not a trace.
Hunt high and low
and you won't find a one,
all of the dragons
but Embers are gone."

The song made Embers feel
very sad. He decided that he
must leave his cave and sail away
to search the world until he
found another dragon. Joseph
was sorry to see his friend go,
but he stood on the shore, waved
goodbye and wished him luck.

For a year and a day Embers
sailed away, then one bright
morning he saw a mermaid
sitting on a rock. She was
combing her long golden hair
and looking at herself in a
mirror. "Have you seen any
dragons?" enquired Embers.
"Of course not!" replied the
mermaid. "Dragons don't exist.
They are entirely mythical."
"I'm not mythical," said
Embers angrily, puffing smoke.
"Then you're not a dragon,"
retorted the mermaid and,
diving down from the rock, she
disappeared into the sea with
hardly a splash.

A few days later Embers sighted land and drifted into shore on a narrow beach. On the other side grew a deep forest. Since he had nothing better to do he decided to explore. He had not gone far when he came upon a unicorn. It was standing quite still by a pool, looking down into the water. "Hello," said Embers. "Have you seen any dragons around here?" "No, I'm afraid not," said the unicorn. "But come and look into the pool." Embers stood by the unicorn's side and looked into the water. He saw the reflection of the tall, tangled trees, but of himself and the unicorn there was no sign. "Makes you wonder, doesn't it?" said the unicorn. Just then there was a sound like thunder and a knight on horseback crashed through the trees. The unicorn disappeared in the twinkling of a thingummybob and left the dragon to face his foe alone. "At last!" cried the knight. "A real, live dragon to fight. Now I can prove my bravery to

Princess Prudence. Prepare to fight, dragon!'' But Embers was an extremely peaceful creature and had no intention of fighting. As the terrible knight lowered his lance and charged, Embers fled and it was the fastest fleeing you ever saw!

Under the sun and under the moon Embers sailed steadily on until at last he came within sight of another shore. And there, on the beach, he found a gryphon. He was building a marvellous sandcastle. "There's no need to tell me," said the

gryphon. "I know the tide will come in and wash it away, but there is so much lovely sand on the beach and I can't think of anything else to do with it, can you?" "No, I suppose not," said Embers. "By the way, have you seen any dragons lately?" "I believe there's a dragon that lives in a cave over there," said the gryphon, pointing out across the sea with his spade.

Embers thanked the gryphon and, filled with excitement, he sailed away. Before long he came upon the cave. It looked very familiar to him, and so it should. It was his own home. Poor Embers could have cried with disappointment, but there, in the mouth of the cave, he saw his friend, the little boy.

"Did you find any dragons?" asked Joseph. "No," sighed Embers. "It seems I'm the only dragon in the world." "Never mind," said Joseph. "Do you know, I think I'm the only Joseph in the world?" The dragon smiled. "Let's play monsters," he said. "I'll chase you." "Great!" shouted Joseph and away he ran across the sands with Embers chasing after him.

The Little People

A BOOK OF FAIRIES ELVES & DWARVES

BY JOHN PATIENCE

King Long Nose

here was once a land which was ruled by a mysterious King who never left his castle. The people of that land supposed that their King must be too proud to come out to see them, but in fact he wasn't at all proud. He was very shy and this was because he had a long nose. "If the people see my long nose," he said to himself, "they will laugh at me and that would be terrible." So the King stayed in his castle, looking at himself in the mirror and feeling unhappy.

I did say the King never left his castle, didn't I? Well, that isn't quite true. Occasionally he would go out for a ride in the forest at night when he thought no-one would see him. Well, one night when he was out riding he noticed a little light glimmering in a bush, and to his amazement he found it to be a fairy. She had somehow managed to get herself tangled up in the branches.. Now, the King was extremely excited by his discovery. He knew well enough that if you catch a fairy you can make her grant a wish. Carefully, he freed her from the bush and held her gently but firmly in his hand. "Let me go!" cried the fairy. "Certainly," replied the King, "but first make my nose shorter." "Granted," said the fairy. Then she touched the King's nose with her wand. There was a loud bang, a puff of coloured smoke and there stood the King. His nose was a little shorter, but so was he! He had turned into an ugly little dwarf. He looked frantically around for the fairy, but there was no sign of her – only the sound of her

mischievous laughter fading into t night. He knew for certain that no-one would believe him now if he claimed to be the King – eve his horse ran away when he approached it. So, sadly he wandered away and at last found himself a cave to live in. There he managed to survive by making himself a bow and hunting the wild animals. Time passed and little changed. Then one morning the King hear someone crying out for help. Rushing out from his cave he found a beautiful Princess. She had been thrown from her horse and was about to be attacked by ferocious bear. Taking good aim with his bow and arrow he shot the bear down dead and ran to help the Princess to her feet. She was so very beautiful that he fel in love with her at first sight, but she seemed to be not in the least bit grateful to him for savin her life. "You are an ugly creature she said. "But I will allow you to accompany me on my way. You may be of some use."

So the dwarf King went along with the beautiful Princess and, before too long, he did prove to be of use to her. They were deep in the dark heart of the forest when they were set upon by a band of wicked elves. They were obviously intent upon carrying off the Princess, but the brave King set about them with a big stick and eventually, after a long battle, he managed to drive them away. Now you might think that this would have softened the Princess's heart towards the King, but no. When she looked at him all she saw was an ugly little dwarf. Yet he had completely lost his heart to her beauty, so he continued to trudge along by the side of her horse.

Eventually the King and the Princess came out at the far side of the forest and continued their journey along a winding road. This led, at length, to a bridge which was guarded by a terrible troll. "I must cross to the other side," said the Princess. "My palace is over there on the mountain top." But the troll would not let them pass. "Leave him to me," said the King and he began to jeer at the terrible creature, making faces at him and calling him names. "Boulder-head, Dumpling-brain, can't catch me!" Then the troll began to chase him and he ran round and round in circles like a little whirlwind, so that, when the troll did at last catch him, he was so dizzy that he could hardly stand up. He reeled around, this way and that – one step forward, two steps back – then, balancing for a moment on the edge of the cliff, over he went, still clutching the King.

You might suppose that that was the end of both of them, but no! Though the troll was killed by the fall, the King landed on the troll's soft tummy, bounced off, struck his head on a rock and lay dazed but not dead on the ground. As for the beautiful Princess, she rode on across the bridge and never gave either of them a second thought!

But the story doesn't end there. Oh no! The King was found by a peasant girl who was out collecting firewood. She was not particularly beautiful. To be honest, she had rather a long nose. However, she had a good heart and when she saw the poor dwarf she thought he was dead and began to cry over him. Her tears welled up from her pure heart and as the first one fell upon the dwarf it immediately washed away the fairy's magic and the King was returned to himself again.

Now the King forgot about the beautiful Princess and fell in love with the peasant girl. They returned together to his palace and not long afterwards they were married. After the ceremony they rode around the city in a golden coach. Everyone cheered and waved and was happy for them and not a single person even noticed their long noses.

The Magic Toy Shop

oby was a problem. Every time his parents took him out anywhere he would pester the life out of them with, "I want this," and "I want that." He was never satisfied until they had bought him a toy or some sweets. Even then he was only happy for a little while. As soon as he had eaten the sweets or grown bored with the toy he would start all over again with, "I want, I want, I want." And when he didn't get what he wanted, he would stamp his feet and throw himself down on the floor of the shop, shouting and screaming at the top of his voice. It was very embarrassing!

Then, one day, someone told Toby about the toy shop where all the toys are magic. "Turn left at the moon and it's second right after midnight," they said. "I want to go there," said Toby. "I want to go to the magic shop." "There's no such place," said Toby's Dad. "Someone's been telling you stories." "No they haven't," shouted Toby. "It's a real place and I want to go there!"

That night Toby dreamed about the magic toy shop, and in his dreams he shouted and screamed so loudly that the little people in fairyland (which is only a cat's whisker away from dreamland) heard his tantrums and decided to do something about them. "Right," they said. "We'll take Toby to the magic toy shop." And so they did. A band of fairies flew in through Toby's open window. They pulled his hair and pinched his nose to wake him up and, before he could shout "Mum!", they whisked him away out into the night and up into the starry sky. Toby was terrified. He was afraid of heights and had to close his eyes tight to stop himself from feeling dizzy. That was a pity because the twinkling lights of the town below them were really beautiful. Never mind, away they flew, left by the moon (who winked his eye) and second right after they heard the midnight chiming of a church clock. And there they were – or rather there was Toby. He opened his eyes to find the fairies had disappeared and he was standing all alone in his pyjamas on a narrow road which curled up and away from him like a wisp of white smoke. At the end of the road, at the top of a hill, stood a tiny, old-fashioned shop, with its window panes twinkling in the sunshine and a rainbow arching above it. It was, of course, the magic toy shop!

A few moments later, slightly out of breath from running up the hill, Toby opened the door of the shop and stepped inside. The doorbell tinkled with a strange sort of faraway sound and Toby felt as if he had walked into a dark little cave. Gradually, however, his eyes grew used to the gloom and he could see that he was indeed standing in the magic toy shop. It was not at all like the toy departments of the

big stores in town. Everything appeared to be muddled up and the toys looked sort of odd too.

Toby had just noticed a great big wooden Noah's Ark and was about to pick up a little lion when it suddenly roared, jumped up and ran away to hide behind a bottle of glass marbles! "Life-like, isn't it?" said a voice. Toby spun round and found the shop-keeper. He was a dwarf no bigger than Toby himself, with a curling, white moustache and a top hat with a train running around it. "And what can I do for you, my lad?" he said. "I want, I want, I want," said Toby, looking greedily around the shop. "Oh, be careful what you want, now," chuckled the dwarf. "I may give it to you." "Great!" cried Toby. "I want that big spinning top." The dwarf smiled strangely, nodded his head and brought Toby the spinning top. It was the old-fashioned kind, made from tin and painted with bright colours. Toby pressed down the handle and it began to spin. It made a weird sort of humming noise which filled up Toby's head. The colours swirled and swirled around and slowly they began to unwind themselves, spinning right off the top and all around Toby like a rainbow whirlpool. "Stop it!" cried Toby. "I feel sick. I want it to stop!" Immediately the top stopped spinning, the colours disappeared

and Toby fell down onto the floor. "I don't want that any more," Toby said angrily. "I want that red drum up there." "Right you are," said the dwarf, climbing a little ladder to bring down the drum Toby had pointed out. "There you are." Toby took the drum and, without a word of thanks, he put the leather strap over his head, picked up the sticks and started to play. BOOM, BOOM, BOOM. It sounded fantastic. He beat it louder – BOOM, BOOM, BOOM. But something was wrong. He couldn't stop. The drumsticks were beating faster and faster and he couldn't put them down. BOOM, BOOM, BOOM. It sounded like thunder. "Stop!" yelled Toby. "I want it to stop!" The dwarf smiled and raised his hand and the drum sticks stopped beating. "Well, now," he said politely. "Is there anything else you want?" "Yes. I want that big rocking horse," said Toby sulkily. "It's yours," said the dwarf. Toby climbed up onto the horse and began to rock. It was fun for a while, but, like all the other toys in the shop, the rocking horse was magic. Suddenly it lifted up its wooden head, whinnied, jumped off its rockers and ran right out of the shop. It galloped around and around the hill, bucking and jumping like a rodeo

horse. Then up it flew into the bright, blue sky, high over the rainbow. "Get me down!" screamed Toby, clinging on for all he was worth. "I want it to stop!" The dwarf whistled and the magic horse flew down from the sky, trotted back into the shop and jumped back onto its rockers and looked exactly like any other rocking horse.

"Well, I've given you everything you wanted," said the dwarf. "Is there anything else now?" "Yes," said Toby. "I want, I want, I want to go home." "No sooner said than done," said the dwarf. Then he clapped his hands together three times and there came a sound like the buzzing of bees. It was the fairies. They flew into the magic toy shop, picked up Toby and carried him away. There was the church clock, still chiming midnight, and there was the old yellow moon winking his eye, and there was the window of Toby's room, and there he was, magically tucked up in bed, fast asleep and dreaming.

The next morning Toby's Mum and Dad took him out shopping. They were astonished. Toby didn't ask for sweets or toys. He didn't say "I want," once. He was as good as gold. Toby's Dad was so pleased with him that he slipped away and bought him a present. When they got home he gave it to Toby. "There you are," he said. "Sometimes you get toys because you *don't* ask for them." Toby opened the present and looked at it in amazement. It was a red drum!

The Fairy Caravan

As I lay sleeping in a field
One Summer's afternoon
I woke to the sound of
Tinkling bells
And the piping of a tune.
And I saw the fairy caravan
Come trooping through the grass
And held my breath
And kept quite still
To watch the fairies pass.

Davey Daydream

re you daydreaming again?" shouted Davey's wife. "That's all you ever do. Why don't you get some work done? Don't you know we have no money and our children are dressed in rags?" Davey sighed, left off his daydreaming and returned to the shoes he was making. A cobbler couldn't make much money even if he worked from sunrise to sunset, and Davey certainly never did that! Often during the day he would put down his hammer, gaze out of the window and let his mind wander off over the mountain. And there he would be a king, living in a beautiful palace, surrounded by servants, eating fine food and wearing fine clothes – and before he knew it the day was gone and no work had been done.

One day, when Davey was feeling stifled in his cobbler's shop, he went out for a walk in the fields and sat himself down upon a little green hill. He had not been there long when a funny little man appeared. "Hello there, Davey

Daydream," he said. How he knew Davey's name Davey couldn't say for he had never seen him before. "What does it feel like to be sitting on top of a fortune?" "What do you mean?" asked Davey. "Don't you know you're sitting on a fairy hill?" replied the little man. "And a fairy hill is filled with fairy gold." Davey thanked the little man and rushed off home to get a spade. Soon he was back at the hill and digging as fast as he could go. "I'll be rich," said Davey to himself. "All my daydreams will come true." But digging was hard work and after a while he grew tired, lay down in the grass to rest and soon fell fast asleep.

The afternoon slipped away. The sun sank down over the hill and the full moon took its place in the sky. Still Davey slept on. Then, as the church clock in the village chimed midnight, something magical happened. A door opened up in the side of the little green hill and out poured a horde of fairies. They sprinkled Davey with fairydust which made him as light as a feather and, while he slept, they carried him away inside the hill. The door closed and once again everything was still. When Davey woke up in fairyland he got the shock of his life, but he need not have worried that the fairies meant him any harm. On the contrary, they loved the company of humans and Davey was treated like a king, even by the King of the Fairies himself. He was brought the finest wines to drink and given food to eat which tasted absolutely out of this world, which of course it was! He was entertained by beautiful fairy music and made as merry as the month of May. It was better than any daydream Davey ever had, and it was real!

But at last Davey began to miss his wife and family and he told the King that he would like to go home. Then, I'm afraid, the fairies changed their tune. "Go home? Never!" cried the King. "You must stay here in fairyland for ever and a day!" "That's a very long time," said Davey. "Please let me go home. I'll do anything you ask." "Very well," replied the King. "You may go home, but first, Cobbler, you must make a pair of shoes for every fairy in fairyland." The King knew very well, of course, that this job would be almost endless. There are as many fairies in fairyland as there are stars in the sky. However, Davey had no choice. He was put in a room with leather and cloth, needle and thread, and he began to work. The shoes were tiny and very difficult to make and soon Davey grew weary. Then, once more, he began to daydream. But this time he didn't dream of being a king – he'd had enough of that. Now his daydreams were of home, his wife and children.

It seemed to Davey that he would never be free. Then one day, when he looked up from his work, there in front of him stood the little old man he had met on the side of the hill. "Never fear, Davey," he said. "Take this leather and make the Fairy King the most beautiful pair of shoes you have ever made in your life. Then, when he has them on his feet, say these magic words –

Pinch, pinch tiny shoes
Pinch his toes to blacks and blues
Make him dance and hop about
Make him squeal and make
him shout."

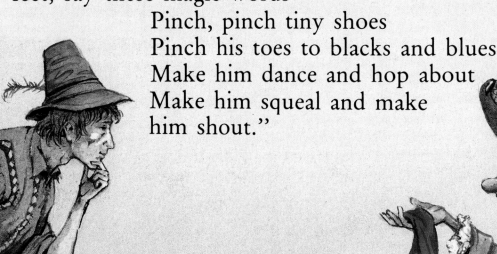

Davey followed the little old man's instructions. He stitched
and sewed and stitched and sewed and he made a pair of
shoes the like of which you have never seen. "They're
perfect," cried the Fairy King. "Let me try them on." He

put them on his tiny feet and strutted around in them like a little peacock. Then Davey spoke the magic words –
Pinch, pinch tiny shoes
Pinch his toes to blacks and blues
Make him dance and hop about
Make him squeal and make him shout.
Immediately the King leapt into the air. "Help!" he shrieked. "The shoes are pinching my toes. Help! Help! Take them off!" The other fairies ran to help but they couldn't even catch the King who couldn't stop himself from dancing around. "Help! Help! Take off the shoes Cobbler. I'll give you anything you want," he cried. "Take off the shoes. Ouch! Ouch!" "Alright," said Davey. "Give me a chest filled with gold." A group of fairies rushed away and returned in a twinkling with a chest of gold coins.

"Now promise to let me go home," said Davey. "I promise! I promise!" shouted the King. Then Davey snapped his fingers in the air and the shoes fell right off the King's feet just as if they were three sizes too big.

Fairies never break their promises – if they do they disappear. So the King kept his promise to Davey who was allowed to leave fairyland with his chest of gold.

Now Davey was well off. Not so well off that he could live like a king, but then he didn't want that any more. His children were well dressed instead of wearing rags and his wife was happy, even when he occasionally still slipped into a daydream. Though what he daydreamed about who can say?

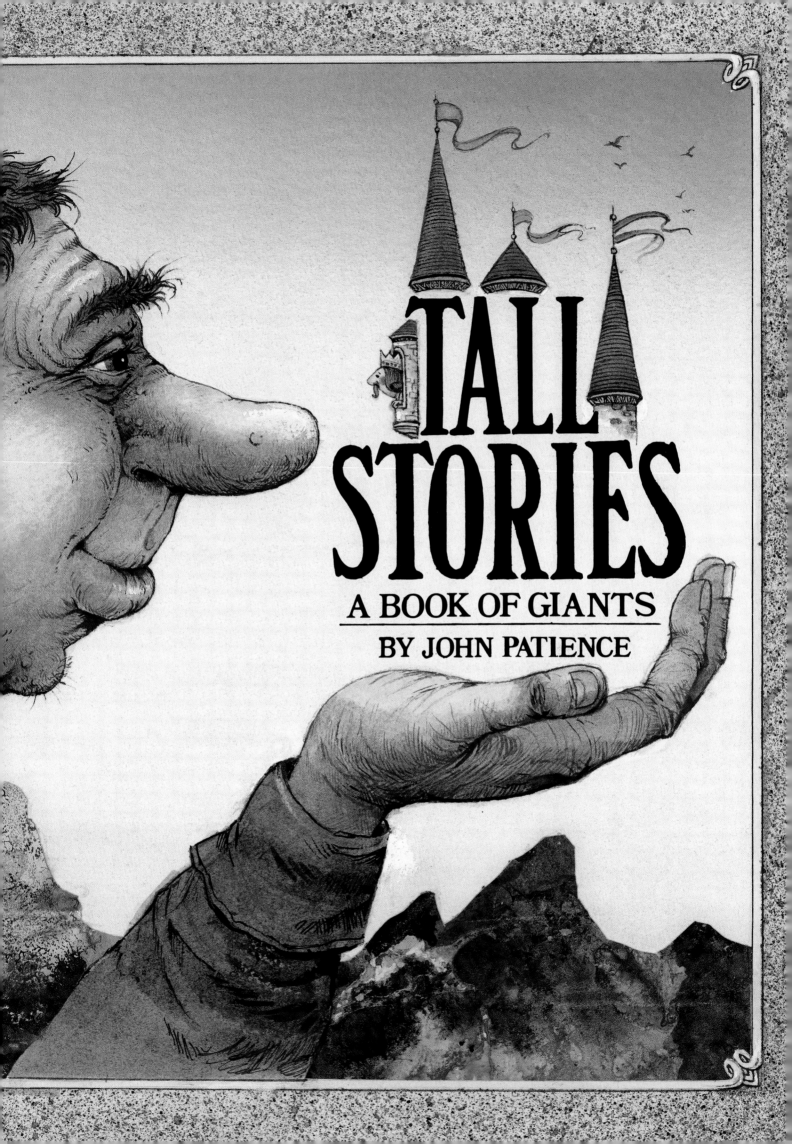

TALL STORIES

A BOOK OF GIANTS

BY JOHN PATIENCE

The Quarrelsome Giants or A Prince of Pigs

Farmer was driving his cart home from market. In the back was a pig which he had failed to sell. What was he going to tell his wife? They had no money left – selling the pig had been their only hope of surviving through the approaching winter. It was not surprising that he had failed to sell the pig, for it was an exceptionally poor looking animal, all skin and bones!

As the farmer was driving along the road he passed by the mouth of a cave and heard a terrible, fierce argument going on inside it. The two voices sounded like thunder and could only belong to a couple of giants. Naturally, the farmer was very much afraid, but it occurred to him that the giants might be interested in buying his pig. After all, what did he have to lose by asking them – only his life and it really wasn't much of a life, scratching around on his miserable little farm. So, mustering up all his courage, the farmer (whose name incidentally was Olaf) climbed down from his cart, put the pig on its lead and gingerly stepped into the cave.

The two giants who (to get all the introductions over with), were brothers named Grumble and Rumble, stopped arguing and eyed the farmer suspiciously. "What do you want?" rumbled Grumble. "And what's that there article you've got with you?" grumbled Rumble. "I'm just a poor farmer," replied Olaf, doffing his hat. "But I happen to own this article, which is actually a pig. A beautiful animal, as I'm sure you will agree. I was wondering if either of you two fine gentlemen would like to buy him from me?" Grumble and Rumble laughed fit to bust. "Buy him from you!" roared Grumble. "We don't buy things, we just takes 'em. And who's going to stop us taking this here pig, eh? Not you, I'm sure." "Quite right," said Olaf, realising that he was in a tricky position. "Buy him? Did I say that? Silly me! He's a present. Of course he is. Take him, please do."

But as he spoke the seed of a plan began to grow in the farmer's mind. "However this is not an ordinary pig," he continued. "He's really a Prince of Pigs and I wouldn't want him to be eaten by just any old giant. I think that the stronger of the two of you should have him." "That sounds fair enough," said Rumble. "You mean me." "No, he doesn't," growled Grumble, "I'm the stronger." "We'll soon see about that!" shouted Rumble, preparing to knock his brother into the middle of next week. "Well now, perhaps a sort of contest should be held to decide the matter," suggested Olaf, soothingly. "Good idea," agreed Grumble. "All right," said Rumble. "I'll win, anyway!"

"Set me a task. I can do anything you can think of," boasted Grumble, flexing his immense muscles. "Very well," said the farmer. "You see that forest over there? Do you think you could clear it away?" "No sooner said than done," said Grumble and it was very nearly true, for Grumble set to with a will. He uprooted the trees with his bare hands and, one after another, tossed them high over the mountain. "Well, what do you think of that?" he asked.

"Absolutely marvellous!" said the farmer. "The pig's mine then," said the giant. "I could do with a bit of a snack after all that hard work."

"Hold on a minute," growled Rumble. "I haven't had my turn yet. Set me a task, Farmer. I can do ten times better than my weakling brother." Well, the cunning old farmer rubbed his chin and scratched his head for a while, and then he said, "I don't suppose you could build a palace over there where your brother pulled up the forest, could you?"

"Couldn't I though!" blustered Rumble. "Just you watch me!" Then, while the farmer looked on in amazement, the giant set to work and, believe it or not, in the twinkling of an eye he had built the most magnificent palace on the face of the earth! "There you are," he said, dusting off his hands. "No problem. The pig is mine." "No it's not!" bellowed his brother. "It's mine. I'm the strongest." "Of course you're not," mocked Rumble. "You're a weed." "I'll teach you a thing or two," thundered Grumble. And the next moment the two monstrosities were locked in a terrible battle.

The fight went on and on all day long, with first one giant getting the upper hand and then the other, until finally, as night was falling, Grumble got the definite advantage. He lifted Rumble up off his feet and, with all his might, he threw him into the air. But Rumble was as fast as lightning and he managed to grab hold of his brother's beard, pulling him up with him. So away they both flew, high into the starry sky, up and up and over the moon. And where they landed I do not know, for they were never seen again.

As for the crafty farmer, he returned to the giants' cave, where he found a hoard of gold and silver and precious stones which he promptly loaded up onto his cart. Then, with the Prince of Pigs sitting up on top of it, away he went, along the winding road, up over the mountain and at last he arrived back home. And there was his dear wife, standing beside the farm house. It had been completely flattened by a tree which his wife assured him had fallen straight out of the sky.

Well, the farmer didn't worry too much about his demolished farm house. He and his wife went to live in the beautiful palace which he had tricked the giant Rumble into building. And what with the giants' treasure, they were very well off to the end of their days. "But what happened to the pig?" you might ask. Well, now he was really the Prince of Pigs for Olaf bought him a real crown and an ermine robe and gave him lots and lots of lovely food to eat so that, in the end, he became quite porky!

When Giants get Sneezes

When giants get sneezes and
Coughs and diseases,
They ought to stay home
And keep warm.
For gigantic sneezes
Can blow down our treeses
And whip up a terrible storm!

The Giant Who Couldn't Sleep

There was once a village where, as night began to fall, people became afraid and would hide themselves away in their houses, bolt their doors, shutter their windows and crawl under their beds. There was a very good reason for this peculiar behaviour, for every evening a great giant would come striding down from the mountains and stomp around the village streets. Over his shoulder he carried an enormous club and upon his face he wore a terrible scowl. "He's looking for someone to gobble up for his supper," mothers would whisper to their children. "Be quiet while he passes."

Every night it was the same story, until one night it was different. As the giant was wandering around the deserted streets he came upon a little boy sitting in a tree. He had climbed up to get his toy aeroplane which had got stuck in the branches, and now he couldn't get down. The little boy, whose name was Ben, trembled with fear when he saw the giant lumbering towards him. He covered his eyes and peeped out between his fingers and saw one of the giant's monstrous great hands reaching out to grab him. Then, to his surprise, he found himself being very gently lifted up out of the tree and set safely down upon the ground.

"Are you g-g-going to eat me?" stammered Ben. "No! Of course not," rumbled the giant. "I'm a vegetarian, and besides, you seem to be a nice little boy. Perhaps we can be friends. Look, here's your aeroplane." The giant carefully picked the toy out of the tree and sent it gliding down to the little boy.

"Everyone says you're fierce," said the boy, looking up at the giant, his eyes round with wonder, "but you're not at all, are you?" "Certainly not!" replied the giant, rather affronted. "Then why do you prowl around the village every night?" "I can't sleep," sighed the giant, and the sigh was such a big heavy sigh that it almost blew Ben off his feet. "Not a wink. And I get so lonely. So I come down into the village looking for company." "Have you tried counting sheep?" asked Ben. "Yes, I have," said the giant, "but I'm not too good at counting. I get up to seven, then I'm not sure what comes next. Is it nine or twelve?" "Fifteen, I think," suggested Ben. "But I think I know a way to make you sleep. Can you take me home? There is something I have to get." "Of course," said the giant, and he picked up

the little boy and sat him upon his shoulder and off they went.

Ben's mother and father were overjoyed to see him back safe and sound, but they were very wary of his new friend, the giant. "Oh dear! He's sure to eat us all up," whispered his mother. "Don't be silly. He's a vegetarian," said Ben. Then, calling over his shoulder, "Don't go away giant. I'll be back in a minute," he ran off to his bedroom. In a few minutes he reappeared, carrying a large book. "I shan't be long," he said reassuringly to his mother and father. "I'm just off to my friend's house." Ben's bewildered parents stood on their doorstep and watched as he climbed up onto the giant's shoulder. "Good-bye!" he called. "See you later." Then the giant lumbered away into the moonlight, his great footsteps shaking the ground beneath him.

The giant climbed higher and higher, picking his way up the winding mountain path and leaving the village so far below them that it looked like a tiny toy. Up and up they went until, at last, they reached an enormous wooden door set into the rock. "Here we are," said the giant, opening the door and stepping inside. "It's not much, but it's home." As a matter of fact, it looked very nice and was a lot more comfortable than you might imagine a giant's cave to be.

Ben hurried the giant along and soon he was climbing into his gigantic bed, a bed big enough for a couple of elephants! "Well," he said, yawning, "what's your plan, Ben?" "It's simple," replied Ben, sitting himself down on the bedside table, under the light of the candle. "I'm going to read you a bedtime story. You'll be off to sleep in no time." And he began to read.

"Once upon a time, long ago, there was a . . ." Ben was right. In no time at all the giant's eyelids grew heavy and he fell into a deep sleep. Then Ben crept quietly out of the cave and made his way home. From then on, Ben read to the giant every night and for a while everything was fine. Then one night everyone in the village was woken by a terrible shout. "Help! Save me, save me!" It was the giant's voice booming down from the mountain. Ben quickly put on his dressing gown and, taking a lamp, climbed up the winding path to the giant's cave. There he found his friend hiding under the bedclothes. "What's the matter?" asked the little boy. "It's the monster. It came to get me!" said the giant, peeping out from under the sheets. "Rubbish!" scoffed Ben. "There's no such thing as monsters. You were having a nightmare." Soon Ben settled his friend down, read him another story and went home. But the next night and the next night and every night for a week the giant woke the village with his shouting. His nightmares were becoming a big problem!

No one knew what to do, then Ben had another brilliant idea. A giant teddy bear! It involved a great deal of work. The farmer brought a cartload of wool to stuff it with. The tailor provided the furry material and Ben's mother and her friends worked until their fingers were sore from stitching. Then, when it was finished, four strong men were needed to help Ben carry the teddy up the mountain – one for each arm and one for each leg!

"Now, Giant," said Ben. "You take this teddy to bed with you and you will never have another bad dream. I know. I take my ted to bed with me and I never have nightmares. Teddies are magic, you see, my mother told me so." Well, the giant was happy now. He snuggled up with his teddy bear and listened to Ben reading him his bedtime story, and fell fast asleep. A sleep with no monsters in it!

"Well, that's that," said Ben, climbing into his own bed. "We can all get some sleep now." "Yes," said his mother as she tucked him in. "It will be very peaceful." But they were both wrong, for no sooner had they spoken, than a new noise came rumbling down from the mountain. It was deafening! It was the sound of the giant snoring, and it shook every bed and rattled every window in the village. But there was nothing anyone could do about that, not even Ben. So, from that day on, they all had to go to bed with cotton wool in their ears!

My Best Friend

My best friend is a giant.
He's bigger than our house.
He's stronger than an elephant,
But quiet as a mouse.
No-one else can see him,
He's invisible, you see,
But he pushes me on the garden swing
And helps me climb the tree.
Sometimes he tells me stories,
As I sit in the palm of his hand,
Of fabulous beasts,
Of fairyland feasts,
Of a mystical, magical land.
But it's a shame when it starts to rain.
He often starts to cry,
'Cause he's too big to come indoors
And we have to say goodbye.

The Greedy Giant and The Miserable Princess

Princess Priscilla was the most beautiful girl in the world. She wore fine clothes, rode around the town in a golden carriage and had scores of servants who pandered to her every whim. Now, you might think that all this would have made her happy, but not a bit of it. The princess was extremely discontented and somehow she managed to make everyone else feel the same way. "I wish something would happen," she would say. "Life is so boring. I wish someone would make me laugh." Well, everyone DID try to make her laugh, but it was no use. She was so miserable that she could reduce the jolliest jester to tears in next to no time. Eventually, the king grew so exasperated with his daughter that he decided to get rid of her by marrying her off to the first prince who could so much as make her smile.

Messengers were sent out from the palace with invitations to all the princes thereabouts to attend a great feast, at which Priscilla would choose a husband.

The day of the feast dawned and the tables in the banqueting hall groaned under the weight of the most succulent, mouth-watering food you can possibly imagine. But before they began to eat, the princes, all seven of them, were introduced to the Princess Priscilla. Unfortunately the princess was looking especially beautiful that day and all the princes lost their hearts to her. But, try as they might, they could not make her smile and they were all rejected. "They are all so dull," sighed the miserable princess.

At that moment things were livened up considerably by a terrible roar and the sound of thunderous footsteps approaching. The great door burst open and in strode the fiercest giant you ever clapped eyes on. He had heard about the feast and was not one to miss the chance of a good meal. Without more ado he sat himself down and began to eat everything in sight. Soon he had polished off the lot! Then, wiping his mouth with the back of his hand, he roared,

"Bring me more food or I'll eat the lot of you." And by the look of his gigantic teeth that would have given him no trouble at all! The servants were sent scurrying down to the kitchen and the fear that they themselves might be the giant's next meal made them double quick about bringing back everything they could find. "This will do very nicely, for the moment," said the giant, talking (as giants often do) with his mouth full.

The giant finished off
his meal then fell fast asleep.
When he awoke a little while
later he was feeling rather peckish.
"Bring me more food!" he bellowed,
"or ..." "We know," sighed the king.
"Or you'll eat the lot of us." But now the
king's larders were empty and food had
to be fetched up from the town, by the cart load.
The greedy giant knew when he was well off and
decided to stay in the palace for a while. The days passed
and his appetite only seemed to grow larger. Cheeses as big
as millstones were brought to him. Loaves as large as
haystacks were baked for him and, in short, every scrap of
food from miles around was delivered up to the giant. Until
at last, there was hardly a crumb of food left in the whole
kingdom and even the mice were starving and as thin as
matchsticks.

Realising that something must be done, the king issued a
proclamation that anyone who could rid the kingdom of the
giant would be granted the beautiful Princess Priscilla's
hand in marriage and he wouldn't even have to make her
smile or be a prince! The princess herself was not too
pleased with this idea, but she was as tired as anyone else of
the giant and so she agreed to the plan.

Now, there was a boy who worked in the king's
kitchens and he had long been in love with Priscilla. He

realised at once that this was his big chance. He promised the king that if he could supply him with the ingredients to make a giant pie, then he could do the trick. Well, one way or another (though, as I have said, there was little food left in the land), the ingredients for the pie were found and the kitchen boy got to work with them. All night long he slaved, stirring up a great, gooey pan of treacle, rolling out an enormous sheet of pastry and finally baking the pie. In the morning, with the help of a number of other servants, he carried the pie up to the banqueting hall and set it before the giant.

The giant's greedy eyes almost popped out of his head when he saw the pie and, opening up his mouth as wide as a cave, he sunk his terrible teeth into it and began to chew, and chew, and chew. The pie was chewy. More than chewy, it was gluey. So gluey that soon the puzzled giant found that his teeth were stuck together. Try as he might, he could not get them apart. He mumbled and grumbled, contorted his face into the most peculiar shapes and turned bright red. He was the funniest thing anyone had ever seen and they all exploded into fits of laughter. Then a most peculiar sound split the air. It was horrible! Everyone looked around to see where the sound was coming from and, to their amazement, they found it was the princess. She was laughing, but what a laugh! How could such a terrible laugh come from such a beautiful person? Priscilla laughed until she wept, pointing her finger at the unfortunate giant and exclaiming, "He's so funny. Just look at him!" Now the giant couldn't get his teeth apart, he couldn't eat anyone and soon he became so embarrassed that he stumbled out of the palace, ran away into the hills and was never seen again.

And did the kitchen lad marry the beautiful Princess Priscilla? No, I'm afraid he didn't. Her horrible laughter had completely put him off. It had put everyone off. But then Priscilla didn't mind. "They're all boring, anyway," she told herself. And maybe they were. And maybe they weren't.

THE END